O'BRIEN panda cubs

PANDA CUBS SERIES
where reading begins

O'BRIEN SERIES FOR YOUNG READERS

 panda cubs

 pandas

 panda tales

 flyers

Cinders

Words: Maddie Stewart
Pictures: Alison Spencer

THE O'BRIEN PRESS
DUBLIN

5179065

For Barbara and Bud

First published 2007 by The O'Brien Press Ltd,
12 Terenure Road East, Dublin 6, Ireland
Tel: +353 1 4923333; Fax: +353 1 4922777
E-mail: books@obrien.ie
Website: www.obrien.ie

ISBN: 978-1-84717-027-9

British Library Cataloguing-in-Publication Data
A catalogue reference for this title is available from the British Library

1 2 3 4 5 6 7 8 9 10
07 08 09 10 11 12

The O'Brien Press receives
assistance from

the arts
council
chomhairle
ealaíon

Typesetting, layout, editing: The O'Brien Press Ltd
Printing: Leo Paper Products Ltd China

Can YOU spot the
panda cub
hidden in the story?

Who lives at number ten
Victoria Street?

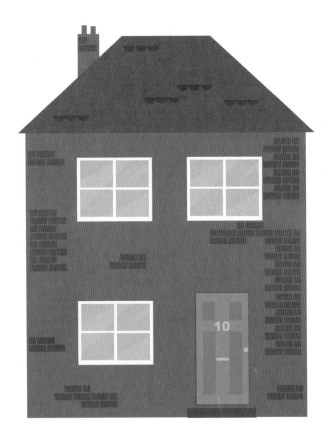

Miss Moll and Cinders,
her old black cat.

At eight o'clock
each morning
Miss Moll goes
out to work.

Cinders stays at home.

She opens the cat flap
and goes out to play
in the garden.

'Miaow!'
She has lots of fun
chasing leaves.

'Miaow!'

She has lots of fun
hunting for
mice.

But she has nobody
to play with.
Poor Cinders is all alone.

At dinnertime
she licks up
all her milk.

And she eats up her

fishy wishy

food.

All by herself.

At six o'clock
Miss Moll comes home.

She sits down on the
big yellow sofa.
Plumpity plump!

Jumpity jump!

Cinders jumps up
and sits on
her knee.

Cinders is so happy that
Miss Moll is home again.

'Poor Cinders,'
said Miss Moll one day.
'You are all alone.
I am going to
find a friend for you.'

Miss Moll went to visit
Sean McGrew.

He had so many pets
that people called him
Sean McZoo.

He had horses and pigs,
donkeys and dogs.

He had geese and goats,
ducks and hens.

He had sheep and cows.

And he had **Tiger**,
a small ginger cat.

Miss Moll put
Tiger in a
basket.
She chuckled
all the way
home.

'Cinders will have a
friend,' she said.
'What a happy cat
she will be.'

But Cinders was **not**
a happy cat.
Cinders did not like Tiger.
She was afraid of him.

Cinders did not want
Tiger in her home.

Cinders wanted Tiger
to go away.

When Cinders went out
Tiger arched
his little ginger back.

He **hissed** at her.

He **spat** at her.
He even **smacked**
her nose.

Home
Sweet
Home

Cinders didn't dare
to go out.
She ran under
the big dresser and hid.

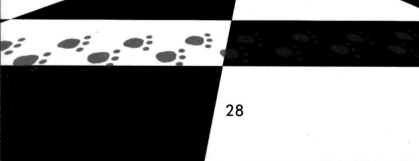

At dinnertime
Cinders went to eat
her fish.

Tiger arched
his little ginger back.

Home
Sweet
Home

He **hissed** at her.

He **spat** at her.

Cinders ran under
the big dresser
and hid.

And Tiger would not let
Cinders sit on
Miss Moll's knee.

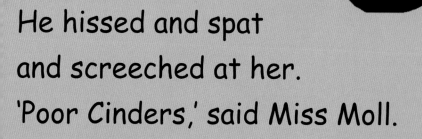

He hissed and spat
and screeched at her.
'Poor Cinders,' said Miss Moll.

Tiger got fatter.

Cinders got thinner.

Tiger got bolder.

Cinders got
more and more afraid.

Miss Moll phoned
Sean McGrew.
'Cinders and Tiger
do not get on at all,'
she said. 'What will I do?'

'Don't worry,' he said,
'I'll bring **Buddy**
around.'

Buddy was a big, big dog.
But Buddy was not
at all brave.

Buddy was **terrified**
of cats.

'Ding-a-ling, a-ling, a-ling,' went the door bell.

Miss Moll picked up Cinders and opened the door.

Buddy saw
Cinders.

'Whu, whu, whu,'
he yelped
in terror,
and he ran away

Cinders puffed out her chest. She inspected her sharp claws.

'What a big, fierce cat I am,' she said.

'The biggest dog
in the world
is terrified of **me**.'

The next time Tiger tried
to scare her
Cinders arched
     her big, black back.

She hissed a fierce hiss.
She showed him
her big, sharp claws.

Tiger backed away.

Soon Cinders and Tiger
were chasing leaves
together,
and hunting mice
together.

When Miss Moll
sat down on the
big yellow sofa,
Cinders and Tiger
curled up beside her.

Now, who lives
at number ten
Victoria Street?

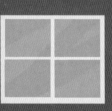

Are they happy?

Yes, they are.